GO FISH!

Story by **Tammi Sauer**   Pictures by **Zoe Waring**

HARPER
An Imprint of HarperCollinsPublishers

Go Fish!
Text copyright © 2018 by Tammi Sauer
Illustrations copyright © 2018 by Zoe Waring
All rights reserved. Manufactured in China.
No part of this book may be used or reproduced in any manner whatsoever without written permission except
in the case of brief quotations embodied in critical articles and reviews. For information address HarperCollins
Children's Books. a division of HarperCollins Publishers. 195 Broadway. New York. NY 10007.
www.harpercollinschildrens.com

ISBN 978-0-06-242155-5

The artist used digital brushes to create the illustrations for this book.
Typography by Rachel Zegar
18 19 20 21 22   SCP   10 9 8 7 6 5 4 3 2 1
❖
First Edition

2

GONE FISHIN'

For Kate, who is a silly goose
—T.K.S.

For Harry and Eilidh, always follow your dreams
—Z.W.

Go ...

...fish!

No fish.

Go fish!

No fish.

Go fish!

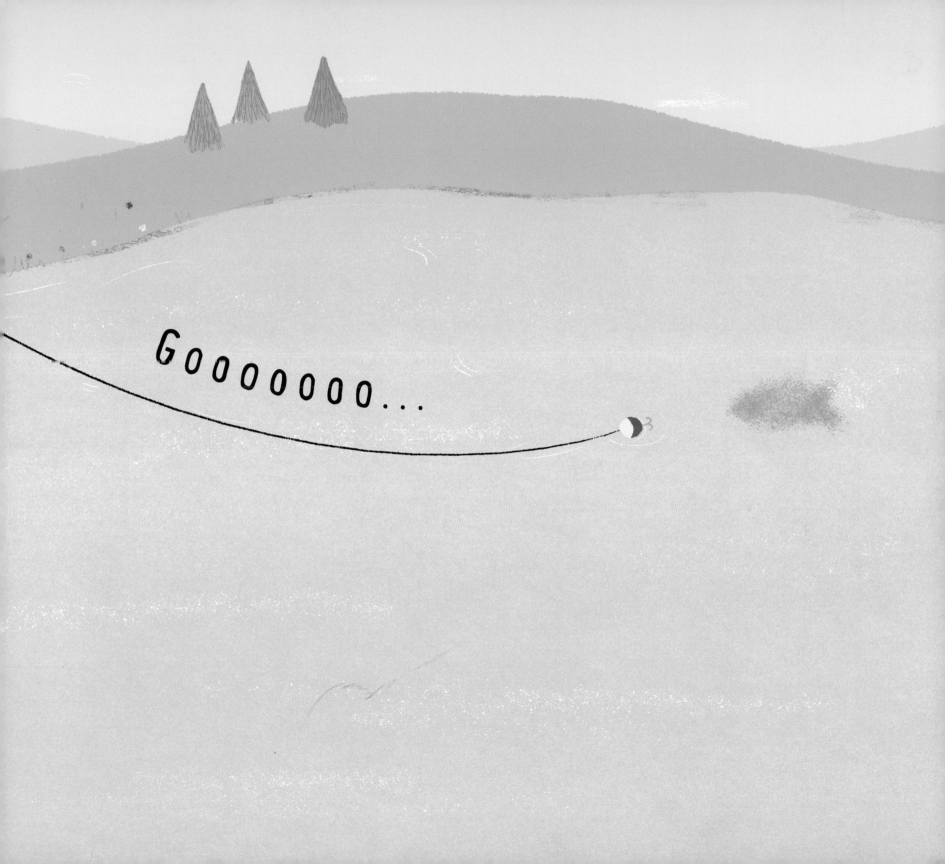

Fish!

WHOA.

No fish!

Here you go, Fish!